D1186604

Over the Hills and Far Away

**For my grandson Joshua and all young rhyme lovers everywhere and
in loving memory of Shelby Anne Wolf, teacher, and Jan Ormerod, artist,
two creative champions of the power of words and pictures to open
our imaginations to the wide wide world and its possibilities
E.H.**

JANETTA OTTER-BARRY BOOKS

Text compilation copyright © Elizabeth Hammill 2014

Illustrations copyright © 2014 Seven Stories, National Centre for Children's Books, except for those copyright © 2014
by the following artists: Ashley Bryan; Eric Carle (see Sources for Illustrations on page 160); Rebecca Cobb;
Nina Crews; Niki Daly; Olivia Lomenech Gill; Mark Hearld; Bill Helin; Shirley Hughes; Catherine Hyde; Kate Leiper;
P.J. Lynch; Jayme McGowan; Andrew Qappik; Niamh Sharkey; Nick Sharratt; Emily Sutton; Mo Willems; Ed Young.
"Bing Buckle" by Ted Dewan copyright © 2014.

First published in Great Britain in 2014 by
Frances Lincoln Children's Books, 74-77 White Lion Street, London N1 9PF
www.franceslincoln.com

All rights reserved

No part of this publication may be reproduced, stored in a retrieval system, or transmitted, in any form, or by any
means, electrical, mechanical, photocopying, recording or otherwise without the prior written permission of the
publisher or a licence permitting restricted copying. In the United Kingdom such licences are issued by the
Copyright Licensing Agency, Saffron House, 6-10 Kirby Street, London EC1N 8TS.

A CIP catalogue record for this book is available from the British Library.

ISBN 978-1-84780-406-8

Printed in China

1 3 5 7 9 8 6 4 2

Over the Hills and Far Away

A treasury of nursery rhymes from around the world

Collected by Elizabeth Hammill

F

FRANCES LINCOLN
CHILDREN'S BOOKS

Contents

In the blue night *(Tohono O'odham)* 10
Michael Chiago

African lullaby *(Akan)* 13
Meshack Asare

Dance, little baby *(English)* 14
Dance to your daddy *(English)* 15
Mick Manning and Brita Granström

Hush, little baby, don't say a word *(American)* 16
Don Cadoret

Hush-a-bye, baby *(English)* 18
Chippewa Lullaby *(Chippewa)* 19
Olivia Lomenech Gill

Lullaby for a girl *(Tsimshian)* 20
Bill Helin

Baby and I *(English)* 22
Pat-a-cake, pat-a-cake *(English)* 23
Yasmeen Ismail

You thumb there, wake up! *(Inuit)* 24
Andrew Qappik

Brow bender *(English)* 26
Earkin-Hearkin *(Yiddish)* 26
Knock at the door *(Chinese American)* 27
Caroline Binch

Moses supposes *(English)* 28
Roses are red *(English)* 29
Bob Graham

What are little boys made of? *(English)* 30
We keep a dog to watch the house
  (Chinese American) 31
Ed Young

Monday's child *(English)* 32
Niki Daly

A wee little boy *(Chinese American)* 34
Polly put the kettle on *(English)* 35
Rebecca Cobb

Diddle diddle dumpling *(English)* 36
Mary, Mary, quite contrary *(English)* 36
Here am I, Little Jumping Joan *(English)* 37
Janey Mac *(Irish)* 37
Niamh Sharkey

Little Miss Muffet *(English)* 38
Clara Vulliamy

Lickle Miss Julie *(Jamaican)* 38
Jenny Bent

Little Miss Tuckett *(American)* 39
Amy Schwartz

Little Miss Muffet *(Australian)* 39
Bruce Whatley

There was a little girl *(English)* 40
Georgie Porgie *(English)* 41
Emma Chichester Clark

Miss Lucy had a baby *(American)* 42
Mo Willems

Little Bo-peep *(English)* 44
Little Boy Blue *(English)* 45
Lydia Monks

Jack and Jill *(English)* 46
Helen Craig

A was an apple pie *(English)*   48
Emily Gravett

One, two, buckle my shoe *(English)*   50
Ted Dewan

One, two, three, four, five *(English)*   52
There once was a fish *(American)*   53
Thomas Docherty

Boys and girls come out to play *(English)*   54
Ring-a-ring o' roses *(English)*   55
Sarah Garland

Abna Babna *(Caribbean)*   56
Eena, deena, dina, do *(South African)*   56
Entry, kentry, cutry, corn *(Anglo-American)*   57
Inty minty tibblety fig *(American)*   57
Pippa Curnick

Little Sally Water *(African American/Caribbean)*   58
Ashley Bryan

Mosquito one, mosquito two *(Trinidadian)*   60
Petrina Wright

I scream, you scream *(American)*   62
Pease porridge hot *(English)*   62
I eat my peas with honey *(American)*   63
If all the world were paper *(English)*   63
Nina Crews

An eagle marching on a line *(Latino)*   64
Little Nancy Etticoat *(English)*   64
A riddle, a riddle, as I suppose *(English)*   64
In marble walls as white as milk *(English)*   65
It has eyes and a nose *(Chinese American)*   65
Michael Foreman

Betty Botter bought some butter *(English)*   66
Peter Piper *(English)*   67
Joel Stewart

Sing, sing *(Anglo-American)*   68
Poussie at the fireside *(Scottish)*   69
Catherine Rayner

Hannah Bantry *(English)*   70
Jack Sprat *(English)*   71
Nick Sharratt

Alas! Alas! For Miss Mackay! *(English)*   72
When I was a little boy *(English)*   73
Mini Grey

Peter, Peter, pumpkin-eater *(English)*   74
I had a little husband *(English)*   75
Emily Sutton

There was an old woman who lived in a shoe
    (English)   76
Jack be nimble *(English)*   77
Jerry Hall *(English)*   77
Paul Hess

Three blind mice *(English)*   78
Hickory, dickory, dock *(English)*   79
Six little mice sat down to spin *(English)*   79
Jessica Ahlberg

Goosey, goosey, gander *(English)*   80
Goosey Goosey Gander *(Australian)*   80
It's raining, it's pouring *(English)*   81
Pamela Allen

Old Mother Hubbard *(English)*   82
Marcia Williams

Higglety, pigglety, pop! *(English)*	84
To market, to market *(English)*	84
Tom, Tom, the piper's son *(English)*	85
Kevin Waldron	
This little pig went to market *(English)*	87
Dis lickle pig go a markit *(Jamaican)*	87
Sian Jenkins	
Mrs Mason *(English)*	88
Gregory Griggs *(English)*	89
Sara Ogilvie	
Oranges and Lemons *(English)*	90
John Lawrence	
The Queen of Hearts *(English)*	92
Pussy cat, pussy cat, where have you been? *(English)*	93
Jane Ray	
Old King Cole *(English)*	94
Hector Protector *(English)*	95
P J Lynch	
Sing a song of sixpence *(English)*	96
I had a little nut tree *(English)*	97
Polly Dunbar	
The lion and the unicorn *(English)*	98
Robert Ingpen	
Yankee Doodle *(American)*	100
The grand old Duke of York *(English)*	101
James Mayhew	
As I was going out one day *(American)*	102
One fine day in the middle of the night *(English)*	103
Piet Grobler	
Simple Simon *(English)*	104
As I was going to St Ives *(English)*	105
David Lucas	
Dickery, dickery, dare *(English)*	107
Miss Mary Mack *(African American/Caribbean)*	107
Jayme McGowan	
There was a crooked man *(English)*	108
Doctor Foster *(English)*	109
Axel Scheffler	
A sunshiny shower *(English)*	110
Whether the weather be fine *(Anglo-American)*	110
Ladybird *(Welsh)*	111
Rain, rain, go away *(English)*	111
Red sky at night *(English)*	111
Rain before seven *(English)*	111
Alan Lee	
January brings the snow *(English)*	112
Catherine Hyde	
Snow, snow faster *(Anglo-American)*	114
The north wind doth blow *(English)*	115
Mark Hearld	
Christmas is a coming *(English)*	116
Little Jack Horner *(English)*	117
Jon Klassen	
In spring I look gay *(English)*	118
I whistle without lips *(Latino)*	119
Lives in winter *(English)*	119
Charlotte Voake	
There was a young farmer of Leeds *(English)*	120
Thistle-seed, thistle-seed *(Chinese American)*	121
Ian Beck	

Puss came dancing out of a barn *(English)* 122
Tom, he was a piper's son *(English)* 123
Laurie Stansfield

All the baby chicks *(Latino)* 124
Baa, baa, black sheep *(English)* 124
This little cow eats grass *(Chinese American)* 125
Pat Hutchins

Rub-a-dub-dub *(English)* 126
Three wise men of Gotham *(English)* 127
There was, was, was *(Latino)* 127
Lucy Cousins

Oh, the train pulled in the station *(American)* 128
Chris Raschka

Who built the ark? *(African American)* 130
Jerry Pinkney

Through the jungle the elephant goes *(Punjabi)* 132
At early morn the spiders spin *(American)* 133
Ladybird, ladybird *(English)* 133
Eric Carle

Kookaburra sits in the old gum tree *(Australian)* 134
Ann James

Fuzzy Wuzzy was a bear *(American)* 135
Shaun Tan

Algy saw a bear *(American)* 135
Gus Gordon

There was an old woman tossed up in a basket
(*English*) 136
Grey goose and gander *(English)* 137
Nicola Bayley

Hey! diddle, diddle *(English)* 139
Satoshi Kitamura

W'en de big owl whoops *(African American)* 140
Don't talk! Go to sleep! *(African American)* 140
Three little ghostesses *(English)* 141
Daniel Minter

White Feathers Along the Edge of the World
(*Tohono O'odham*) 142
Song of Red Fox *(Wintu)* 143
Allison Francisco

Twinkle, twinkle, little star *(English)* 144
Star light, star bright *(English)* 145
Shirley Hughes

Wee Willie Winkie *(Scottish)* 146
Come, let's to bed *(English)* 146
Up the wooden hill *(English)* 147
Go to bed first *(English)* 147
Kate Leiper

Hush-a-bye *(African American)* 149
You are weeping *(Maori)* 149
Holly Sterling

Bed is too small for my tiredness *(American)* 150
Pamela Zagarenski

About the artists 152
Index of First Lines 156
Seven Stories, National Centre for Children's Books 159
Sources 160

Introduction

Nursery rhymes have enlivened my life for as long as I can remember. Their music, beat, rhythm, repetition and rhyme still extend an irresistible invitation to my senses today. The astonishing variety of subject, mood, scene, landscape and character discovered in these tiny masterpieces of verse still delight. The ways in which they have outlasted their oral origins as street cries, folk songs, political satire, remnants of custom and proverb, and been polished into perfect form over time, now fascinate me as does the enriching of this canon with English translations of verse for the young from other cultural traditions.

The rhymes I grew up with came from 'Mother Goose' – a dame first known for telling Charles Perrault's fairy stories, but then, round about 1780, for the singing of nursery rhymes in the fifty-one 'songs and lullabies' of her historic *Mother Goose's Melody, or, Sonnets for the Cradle*. My Mother Goose appeared as a transplant surrounded by newer American homegrown verses in *The Golden Songbook* (1945). Here I was introduced to the world, and who I might be in it, and taken into the land of make-believe. From lullabies to counting rhymes, to riddles and miniature but memorably dramatic or nonsensical stories, these rhymes, once learned, have stayed with me for a lifetime. Who can forget such characters as Peter Piper, Little Miss Muffet or Old Mother Hubbard, or such delicious absurdities as a cow jumping over the moon or an old woman putting her children to bed in a shoe?

When I moved to England with my young family, I became aware of how Mother Goose rhymes are borderless – migrating with ease, begetting intriguing cultural variants along the way. In my work as a children's bookseller and critic, I grew increasingly fascinated by rhyme and language in motion. I discovered Mother Goose rhymes in collections from across the English-speaking world being given new life outside Britain. I came upon anthologies of parallel rhymes and verse that have entered and enhanced the English lexicon from Asia, the Caribbean, and African, Native American and Hispanic cultures and elsewhere, often in single-culture collections. Children, after all, are children everywhere and are entertained and comforted by the same things. I have listened with pleasure to the diverse voices that speak in verse to the very young. Nowhere, however, have I found a wide-ranging collection that sits these translated and newer voices alongside Mother Goose favourites and injects fresh life into them – providing a genuine intercultural experience.

Here, then, is my collection for you. It not only celebrates such rhyme and verse but also the art of illustration and the many distinctive voices that speak to the young in pictures. Created to benefit Seven Stories, Britain's National Centre for Children's Books, which I initiated and co-founded, this anthology features illustrations by seventy-seven artists from across the English-speaking world. Some established, some emerging, including the winners of the Frances Lincoln/Seven Stories Illustration Competition for UK art students, all have enthusiastically and generously contributed the artwork for this book, and donated it and their work-in-progress to the Seven Stories' Collection. Finding and getting to know these artists and their work, so that I could match verse and illustrator culturally, temperamentally and stylistically, has been a bracing challenge. I have been delighted by the wit, imagination, multiple perspectives, interpretative takes, experimentation in style and sense of 'joy', as Ashley Bryan put it, that pervade the images you find here.

I invite you now to travel with me 'over the hills and far away' on an adventure in language, image and imagination. Along the way, you will find new sounds, new sights, new ways with words, new horizons and a new delight in poetry and art. Share and enjoy!

Elizabeth Hammill

How shall I begin my song
In the blue night that is settling?
I will sit here and begin my song.

Tohono O'odham

Someone would like to have you for her child,
    but you are mine.
Someone would like to rear you on a costly mat,
    but you are mine.
Someone would like to place you on a camel blanket,
    but you are mine.
I have you to rear on a torn old mat.
Someone would like to have you for her child,
    but you are mine.

Akan

Dance, little baby, dance up high,
Never mind, baby, mother is nigh;
Crow and caper, caper and crow,
There, little baby, there you go.
Up to the ceiling, down to the ground,
Backwards and forwards, round and round;
So dance, little baby, and mother will sing,
With a high cockolorum and tingle, ting, ting.

English

Trigger Fish

Pickerel

Atlantic Mackerel

Atlantic Salmon

European Perch

Sea Robin

Flying Fish

Cuttlefish

Pike

European Plaice

John Dory

Atlantic Cod

Dance to your daddy,
My little babby,
Dance to your daddy,
My little lamb.

You shall have a fishy
In a little dishy,
You shall have a fishy
When the boat comes in.

English

15

Hush, little baby, don't say a word,
Mama's goin' to buy you a mocking-bird.

If that mocking-bird don't sing,
Mama's goin' to buy you a diamond ring.

If that diamond ring turns brass,
Mama's goin' to buy you a looking glass.

If that looking glass gets broke,
Mama's goin' to buy you a billy goat.

If that billy goat won't pull,
Mama's goin' to buy you a cart and bull.

If that cart and bull turn over,
Mama's goin' to buy you a dog named Rover.

If that dog named Rover won't bark,
Mama's goin' to buy you a horse and cart.

If that horse and cart fall down,
You'll still be the sweetest little baby in town.

American

16

The Mayflower
1620–1621

Newtoncoon:

Hush - a - bye, baby,
On the tree top,
When the wind blows
The cradle will rock;
When the bough breaks
The cradle will fall,
Down will come baby,
Cradle, and all.

English

Little baby, sleep,
Mother swings your hammock low;
Little birds are asleep in their
nest.
Way, way, way, way, way,
Way, way, way, way,
way, way, way,
Little baby with nothing
to fear.

Chippewa

Olivia Lomenech Gill.

The little girl was born to gather wild roses.

a – ho – ho – he – he hi – a.

The little girl was born to dig wild rice.

a – ho – ho – he – he hi – a.

The little girl was born to get hemlock sap.

a – ho – ho – he – he hi – a.

The little girl was born to pick strawberries.

a – ho – ho – he – he hi – a.

The little girl was born to pick soapberries.

a – ho – ho – he – he hi- a.

The little girl was born to pick elderberries.

a – ho – ho – he – he hi – a.

The little girl was born to gather wild roses.

a – ho -ho – he – he hi – a.

a – he – he – he a – he – he -he a – hi

a – he – he – he a – he – he -he a – hi

a hye – ha-ye he – he ha he

he – he – he – a hi

Tsimshian laughing song

Tsimshian artist Bill Helin, his parents, and their parents before them were sung this "laughing" or "silly" song by their elders. Believing that children should be happy and hopeful, despite the hard village life that awaits them as they grow up, singers imagine a day when the little girl will gather wild roses and experience a moment in her life "as sweet and as beautiful as the roses"– roses she might have found on Rose Island near the remote northern coastal community of Lax Kw'alaams.

Baby and I
Were baked in a pie,
The gravy was wonderful hot.
We had nothing to pay
To the baker that day
And so we crept out of the pot.

English

22

Pat-a-cake, pat-a-cake,
Baker's man.
Bake me a cake
As fast as you can.
Pat it and prick it
And mark it with B,
And put it in the oven
For Baby and me.

English

You thumb there, wake up!

The kayak-rowers are about to leave you!

Forefinger there, wake up!

The umiak-rowers are about to leave you!

Middle finger there, wake up!

The wood-gatherers are about to leave you!

Ring finger there, wake up!

The berry-gatherers are about to leave you!

Little finger there, wake up!

The crake-heather-gatherers are about to leave you!

Inuit finger game

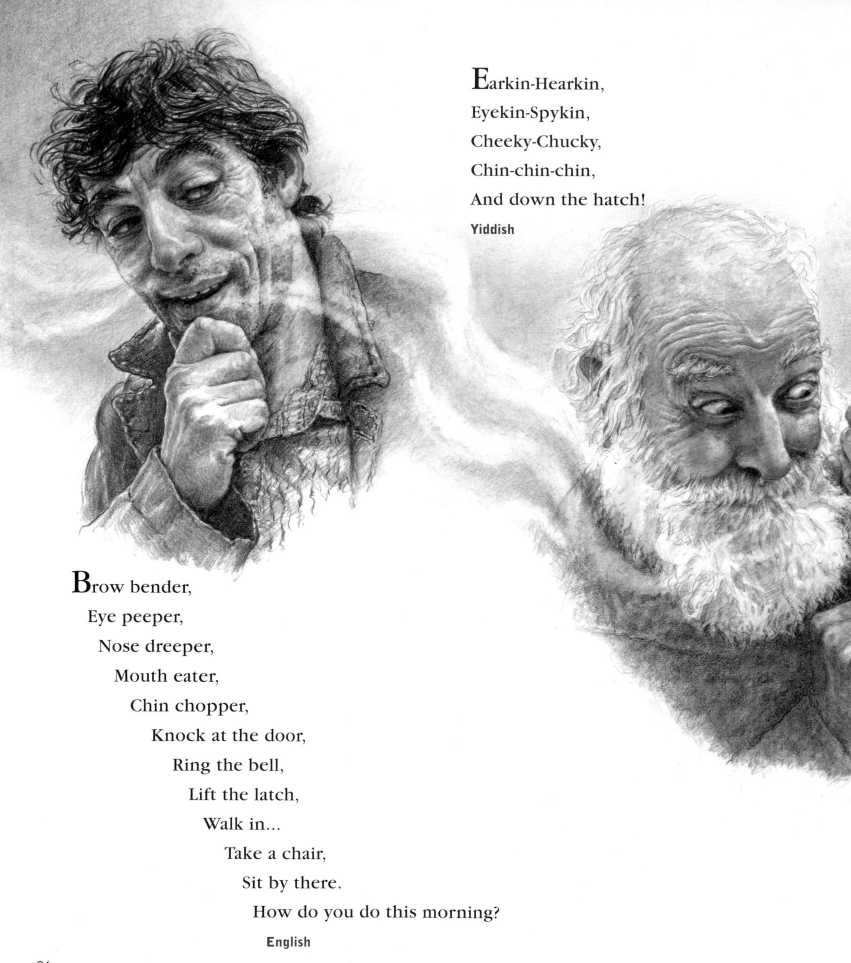

Earkin-Hearkin,
Eyekin-Spykin,
Cheeky-Chucky,
Chin-chin-chin,
And down the hatch!

Yiddish

Brow bender,
Eye peeper,
Nose dreeper,
Mouth eater,
Chin chopper,
Knock at the door,
Ring the bell,
Lift the latch,
Walk in...
Take a chair,
Sit by there.
How do you do this morning?

English

Knock at the door,
   See a face,
      Smell an odor,
         Hear a voice,
            Eat your dinner,
               Pull your chin, or
                  Ke-chih,
                     Ke-chih.

Chinese American

Moses supposes his toeses are roses,
But Moses supposes erroneously.
For Moses he knowses his toeses aren't roses,
As Moses supposes his toeses to be.

English

Roses are red.
Violets are blue.
Sugar is sweet
And so are you.

English

Bob Graham

What are little boys made of, made of,
What are little boys made of?
Snips and snails, and puppy-dogs' tails;
And that's what little boys are made of.

What are little girls made of, made of,
What are little girls made of?
Sugar and spice, and all that's nice;
And that's what little girls are made of.

English

We keep a dog to watch the house,
A pig is useful, too;
We keep a cat to catch a mouse,
But what can we do
With a girl like you?

Chinese American

Monday's child is fair of face,

Tuesday's child is full of grace,

Wednesday's child is full of woe,

Thursday's child has far to go,

32

Friday's child
is loving
and giving,

Saturday's child works
hard for a living,

But the child
that's born on the
Sabbath day
Is bonny and blithe
and good and gay.

English

Photography by Magritte Brink

Niki Daly

A wee little boy
Has opened a store,
In two equal parts
Is his front door,

A wee little table,
A wee little chair,
And ebony chop-sticks
And plate are there.

Chinese American

34

Polly put the kettle on,
Polly put the kettle on,
Polly put the kettle on.
We'll all have tea.

Sukey take it off again,
Sukey take it off again,
Sukey take it off again.
They've all gone away.

English

Diddle, diddle, dumpling, my son John,
Went to bed with his trousers on;
One shoe off, and one shoe on,
Diddle, diddle, dumpling, my son John.

English

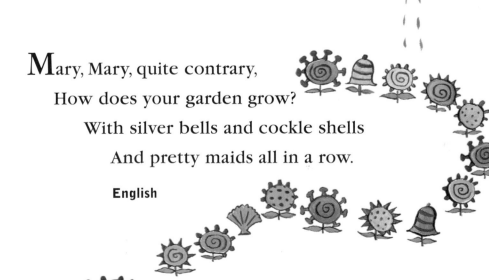

Mary, Mary, quite contrary,
How does your garden grow?
With silver bells and cockle shells
And pretty maids all in a row.

English

Here am I,
Little Jumping Joan,
When nobody's with me,
I'm all alone.

English

Janey Mac, me shirt is black,
What'll I do for Sunday?
Go to bed and cover me head
And not get up till Monday.

Irish

Niamh Sharkey   37

Little Miss Muffet
Sat on a tuffet,
Eating her curds and whey.
There came a big spider,
Who sat down beside her
And frightened Miss Muffet away.

English

Lickle Miss Julie
Kotch pon ar stoolie,
An nyam wan ripe bombay;
Den bredda Anancy
Come frighten de pickney
An tief de ripe mango away.

Jamaican

Little Miss Tuckett
Sat on a bucket,
Eating some peaches and cream.
There came a grasshopper
And tried hard to stop her,
But she said, "Go away, or I'll scream."

American

Little Miss Muffet
Arose from her tuffet
To box with the old kangaroo.
There came a big wombat
To join in the combat,
And Little Miss Muffet withdrew.

Australian

39

There was a little girl,
and she had a little curl
Right in the middle
of her forehead;

When she was good,
she was very, very good,
But when she was bad,
She was horrid.

English

40

Georgie Porgie, pudding and pie,
Kissed the girls and made them cry.
When the boys came out to play.
Georgie Porgie ran away.

English

41

Miss Lucy had a baby,
She named him Tiny Tim,
She put him in the bathtub
To see if he could swim.

He drank up all the water,
He ate a bar of soap,
He tried to eat the bathtub,
But it wouldn't go down his throat.

Miss Lucy called the doctor,
Miss Lucy called the nurse,
Miss Lucy called the lady
With the alligator purse.

In came the doctor,
In came the nurse,
In came the lady
With the alligator purse.

"Mumps," said the doctor,
"Measles," said the nurse,
"Chicken pox," said the lady
With the alligator purse.

Out went the doctor,
Out went the nurse,
Out went the lady
With the alligator purse.

American

Little Bo-peep has lost her sheep,
And doesn't know where to find them.
Leave them alone, and they'll come home,
Bringing their tails behind them.

Little Bo-peep fell fast asleep,
And dreamt she heard them bleating.
But when she awoke, she found it a joke,
For they were still a-fleeting.

Then up she took her little crook,
Determined for to find them.
She found them indeed, but it made her heart bleed,
For they'd left their tails behind them.

It happened one day, as Bo-peep did stray
Into a meadow hard by,
There she espied their tails side by side,
All hung on a tree to dry.

She heaved a sigh, and wiped her eye,
And over the hillocks went rambling,
And tried what she could, as a shepherdess should,
To tack again each to its lambkin.

English

44

Little Boy Blue,
Come blow your horn,
The sheep's in the meadow,
The cow's in the corn;
But where is the boy
Who looks after the sheep?
He's under a haycock,
Fast asleep.
Will you wake him?
No, not I,
For if I do,
He's sure to cry.

English

45

Jack and Jill
Went up the hill
To fetch a pail of water.

Jack fell down
And broke his crown
And Jill came tumbling after.

Then up Jack got,
And home did trot,
As fast as he could caper.

He went to bed,
To mend his head
With vinegar and brown paper.

When Jill came in,
How she did grin
To see Jack's paper plaster.

Her mother, vexed,
Did beat her next,
For laughing at Jack's disaster.

Now Jack did laugh
And Jill did cry,
But her tears did soon abate,

Then Jill did say
That they should play
At see-saw across the gate.

English

Helen Craig 47

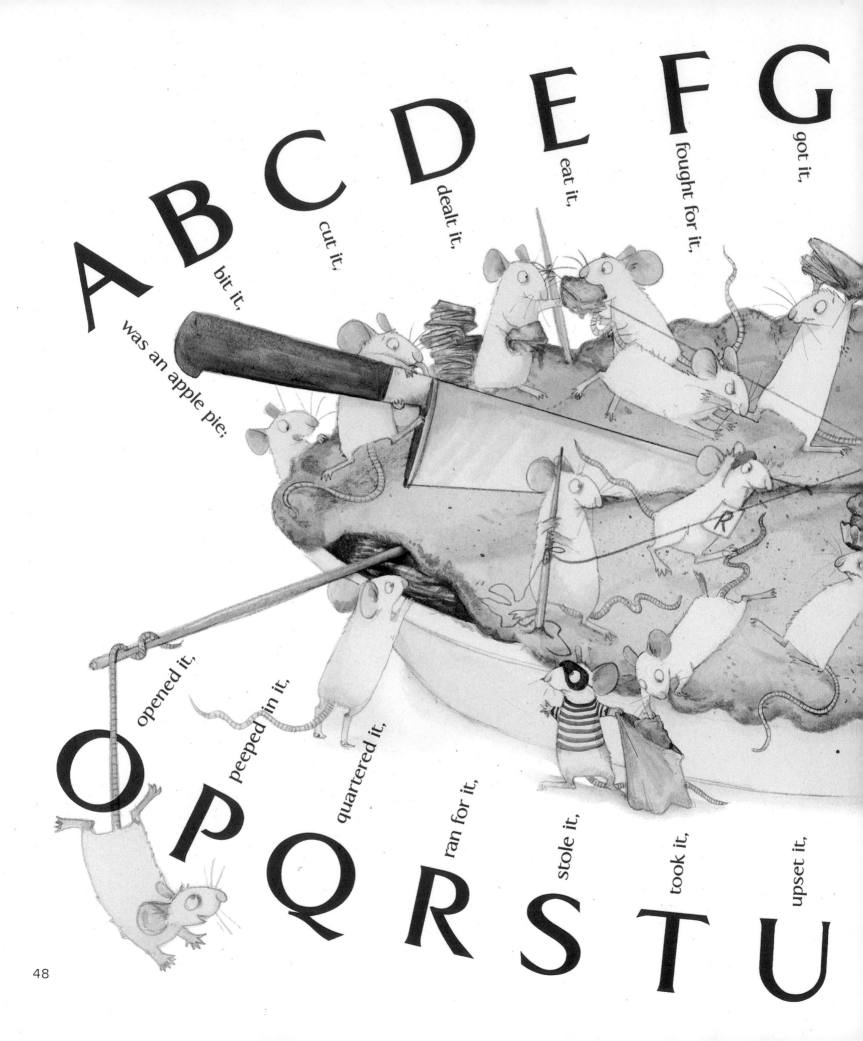

A

B bit it,

was an apple pie;

C cut it,

D dealt it,

E eat it,

F fought for it,

G got it,

O opened it,

P peeped in it,

Q quartered it,

R ran for it,

S stole it,

T took it,

U upset it,

H had it,

I inspected it,

J jumped for it,

K kept it,

L longed for it,

M mourned for it,

N nodded at it,

viewed it,

wanted it,

V W X Y Z and ampersand

All wished for a piece in hand.

English

Bing
Buckle ™
by Ted Dewan

1 2 Buckle my shoe.

3 4 Whack the door.

5 6 Carrot sticks.

7 8

dak!

shut the gate!

9 10

A big fat hen.

English

Licensed by Acamar Films Ltd

One, two, three, four, five,

Once I caught a fish alive,

Six, seven, eight, nine, ten,

Then I let it go again.

Why did you let it go?

Because it bit my finger so.

Which finger did it bite?

This little finger on the right.

English

There once was a fish.
(What more could you wish?)
He lived in the sea.
(Where else would he be?)
He was caught on a line.
(Whose line if not mine?)
So I brought him to you.
(What else should I do?)

American

Boys and girls come out to play,
The moon doth shine as bright as day,
Leave your supper, and leave your sleep,
And join your playfellows in the street.
Come with a whoop, and come with a call,
Come with a good will or not at all.

Up the ladder and down the wall,
A half-penny loaf will serve us all;
You find milk, and I'll find flour,
And we'll have a pudding in half an hour.

English

54

Ring-a-ring o' roses,
A pocket full of posies,
A-tishoo! A-tishoo!
We all fall down.

The cows are in the meadow
Lying fast asleep;
A-tishoo! A-tishoo!
We all get up again.

English

Abna Babna
Lady-Snee
Ocean potion
Sugar and tea
Potato roast
And English toast
Out goes she.

Caribbean counting-out rhyme

Eena, deena, dina, do.
Catla, weena, wina, wo.
Each peach, pear, plum
Out goes Tom Thumb.

South African counting-out rhyme

Entry, kentry, cutry, corn,
Apple seed and apple thorn.
Wire, briar, limber lock,
Three geese in a flock.
One flew east, one flew west,
One flew over the cuckoo's nest.
O-U-T spells out goes she.

Anglo-American counting-out rhyme

Inty minty tibblety fig,
Deema dima doma jig,
Howchy powchy domi nowchy,
Hom tom tout,
Olligo bolliga boo,
Out goes YOU.

American counting-out rhyme

Little Sally Water,
Sitting in a saucer,
Crying and a-weeping for someone to come.
Rise, Sally, rise, Sally,
Wipe your weeping eyes, Sally.
Fly to the East, Sally,
Fly to the West, Sally,
Fly to the very one that you love the best.

Put your hands on your hips,
Let your backbone shake,
Shake it to the East,
Shake it to the West,
Shake it to the very one that
you love the best.

Caribbean clapping rhyme

Mosquito one,
Mosquito two,
Mosquito jump in de callaloo.

Mosquito three,
Mosquito four,
Mosquito fly out de ol' man door.

PETRINA
WRIGHT

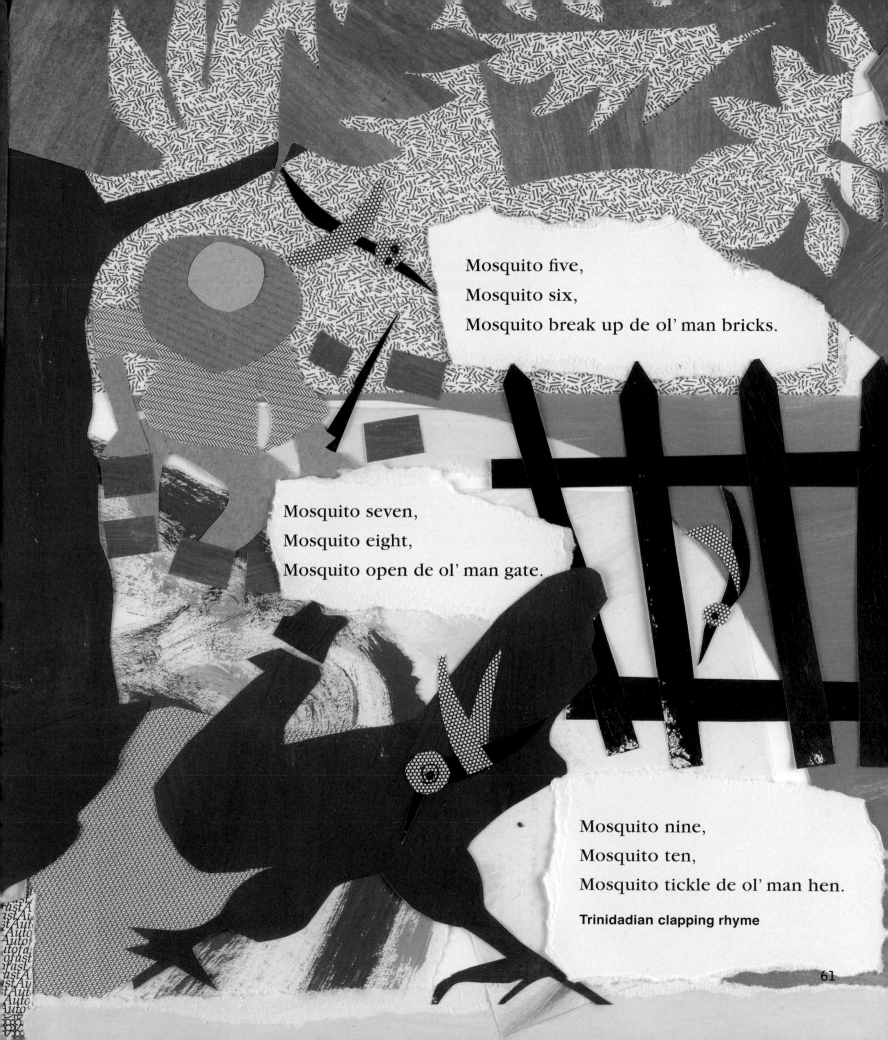

Mosquito five,
Mosquito six,
Mosquito break up de ol' man bricks.

Mosquito seven,
Mosquito eight,
Mosquito open de ol' man gate.

Mosquito nine,
Mosquito ten,
Mosquito tickle de ol' man hen.

Trinidadian clapping rhyme

61

I SCREAM,

YOU SCREAM,

WE ALL SCREAM

FOR ICE CREAM.

American

Pease porridge hot,
Pease porridge cold,
Pease porridge in the pot,
Nine days old.
Some like it hot,
Some like it cold,
Some like it in the pot,
Nine days old.

English

I eat my peas with honey;
I've done it all my life.
It makes the peas taste funny,
But it keeps them on the knife.

American

If all the world were paper,
And all the sea were ink,
If all the trees were bread and cheese,
What should we have to drink?

English

An eagle marching on a line,
Its beak before, its eyes behind.

Latino

Scissors

Little Nancy Etticoat,
With a white petticoat,
And a red nose;
She has no feet or hands,
The longer she stands
The shorter she grows.

English

A candle

A riddle, a riddle, as I suppose,
A hundred eyes, and never a nose.

English

A potato

64

It has eyes and a nose
But has not breathed since birth;
It cannot go to heaven
And will not stay on earth.

Chinese American

A dragon kite

In marble walls as white as milk,
Lined with a skin as soft as silk,
Within a fountain crystal-clear,
A golden apple doth appear,
No doors there are to this stronghold,
Yet thieves break in and steal the gold.

English

An egg

Betty Botter bought some butter,
But, she said, the butter's bitter;
If I put it in my batter
It will make my batter bitter,
But a bit of better butter
Will make my batter better.
So she bought a bit of butter
Better than her bitter butter,
And she put it in her batter
And the batter was not bitter,
So 'twas better Betty Botter
Bought a bit of better butter.

English

Peter Piper picked a peck of pickled peppers;
A peck of pickled peppers Peter Piper picked;
If Peter Piper picked a peck of pickled peppers,
Where's the peck of pickled peppers Peter Piper picked?

English

Sing, sing,
What shall I sing?
The cat's run away
With the pudding string.

Do, do,
What shall I do?
The cat's run away
With the pudding, too!

Anglo-American

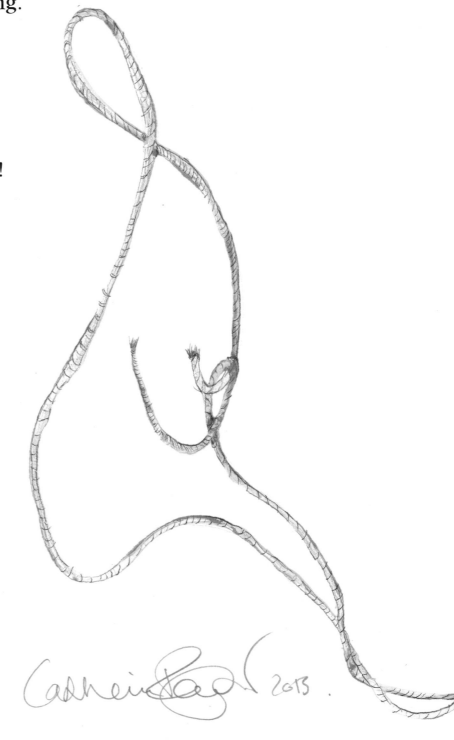

Poussie at the fireside,
Suppin up brose;
Doon cam a cinder,
And brunt Poussie's nose.

"Echt!" cried Poussie,
"That's nae fair!"
"It's a' hex," said the cinder,
"Ye shouldna hae been there."

Scottish

69

Hannah Bantry, in the pantry,
Gnawing at a mutton bone.
How she gnawed it,
How she clawed it,
When she found herself alone.

English

Jack Sprat could eat no fat,
His wife could eat no lean,
And so, betwixt them both, you see,
They licked the platter clean.

English

71

Nick Sharratt

Alas! Alas! For Miss Mackay!
Her knives and forks have run away;
And when the cups and spoons are going,
She's sure there is no way of knowing.

English

When I was a little boy,
I washed my mammy's dishes;
I put my finger in my eye,
And pulled out golden fishes.

My mother called me good boy,
And bid me do't again;
I put my finger in my eye,
And got threescore and ten.

English

Peter, Peter, pumpkin-eater,
Had a wife, and couldn't keep her;
He put her in a pumpkin shell,
And there he kept her very well.
English

I had a little husband
No bigger than my thumb;
I put him in a pint pot
And there I bid him drum.
I bought a little horse
That galloped up and down;
I bridled him, and saddled him
And sent him out of town.
I gave him a pair of garters
To garter up his hose,
And a little silk handkerchief
To wipe his snotty nose.

English

Emily Sutton

There was an old woman
Who lived in a shoe,
She had so many children
She didn't know what to do;
She gave them some broth
Without any bread,
And whipped them all soundly
And put them to bed.

English

Jack be nimble,
Jack be quick,
Jack jump over
The candle stick.

English

Jerry Hall,
He is so small,
A rat could eat him
Hat and all.

English

Paul Hess

77

Three blind mice,
Three blind mice,

See how they run!
See how they run!

They all ran after
the farmer's wife,

Who cut off their tails
with a carving knife.

Did you ever see
such a sight in your life,
As three blind mice?

English

Hickory, dickory, dock,

The mouse ran up the clock.

The clock struck one,

The mouse ran down,

Hickory, dickory, dock.

English

Six little mice sat down to spin;

Pussy passed by and she peeped in.

What are you doing, my little men?

Weaving coats for gentlemen.

Shall I come in and cut off your threads?

No, no, Mistress Pussy, you'd bite off our heads.

Oh, no, I'll not; I'll help you spin.

That may be so, but you can't come in.

English

Goosey, goosey, gander,
Whither shall I wander?
Upstairs and downstairs
And in my lady's chamber.
There I met an old man
Who would not say his prayers.
I took him by the left leg
And threw him down the stairs.

English

Goosey Goosey Gander,
Whither do you wander?
Your place is in the poultry yard
And not on the verandah.

Australian

It's raining, it's pouring,
The old man is snoring.
He got into bed
And bumped his head,
And couldn't get up in the morning.

English

81

Higglety, piggglety, pop!
The dog has eaten the mop;
The pig's in a hurry,
The cat's in a flurry,
Higglety, piggglety, pop!

English

To market, to market,
To buy a fat pig,
Home again, home again,
Jiggety-jig!
To market, to market,
To buy a fat hog,
Home again, home again,
Jiggety-jog!

English

Tom, Tom, the piper's son,
Stole a pig and away he run;
The pig was eat and Tom was beat,
And Tom went howling down the street.

English

Geulins

This little pig went to market,
This little pig stayed at home,
This little pig had roast beef,
This little pig had none,
And this little pig cried, 'Wee-wee-wee!'
All the way home.

English

Dis lickle pig go a markit,
Dis lickle pig tan a yaad,
Dis lickle pig nyam curry goat,
Dis lickle pig got nun,
Dis lickle pig holla, 'Wahi, wahi, wah!'
All de way a im yaad.

Jamaican

Mrs Mason
bought a basin,

Mrs Tyson said,
What a nice'un,
What did it cost?
said Mrs Frost,
Half a crown,
said Mrs Brown,
Did it indeed?
said Mrs Reed,
It did for certain,
said Mrs Burton.
Then Mrs Nix
up to her tricks
Threw the basin
on the bricks.

English

Gregory Griggs, Gregory Griggs,
Had twenty-seven different wigs.
He wore them up, he wore them down,
To please the people of the town;
He wore them east, he wore them west,
But he never could tell which he loved the best.

English

89

Gay go up and gay go down,
To ring the bells of London town.

Bull's eyes and targets,
Say the bells of St Marg'ret's.

Brickbats and tiles,
Say the bells of St Giles'.

Halfpence and farthings,
Say the bells of St Martin's.

Oranges and lemons,
Say the bells of St Clement's.

Pancakes and fritters,
Say the bells of St Peter's.

Two sticks and an apple,
Say the bells of Whitechapel.

Pokers and tongs,
Say the bells of St John's.

Kettles and pans,
Say the bells of St Ann's.

Old Father Baldpate,
Say the slow bells of Aldgate.

You owe me ten shillings,
Say the bells of St Helen's.

When will you pay me?
Say the bells of Old Bailey.

When I grow rich,
Say the bells of Shoreditch.

Pray when will that be?
Say the bells of Stepney.

I am sure I don't know,
Says the great bell of Bow.

Here comes a candle to light you to bed,
Here comes a chopper to chop off your head.

English

The Queen of Hearts
She made some tarts,
All on a summer's day;

The Knave of Hearts
He stole those tarts,
And took them clean away;

The King of Hearts
Called for the tarts,
And beat the knave full sore;
The Knave of Hearts
Brought back the tarts,
And vowed he'd steal no more.

English

Pussy cat, pussy cat, where have you been?
I've been to London to look at the queen,
Pussy cat, pussy cat, what did you there?
I frightened a little mouse under her chair.

English

Old King Cole
Was a merry old soul,
And a merry old soul was he.
He called for his pipe,
And he called for his bowl,
And he called for his fiddlers three.

Every fiddler he had a fiddle,
And a very fine fiddle had he;
Oh, there's none so rare
As can compare
With King Cole and his fiddlers three.

English

Hector Protector was dressed all in green;
Hector Protector was sent to the Queen.
The Queen did not like him,
No more did the King;
So Hector Protector was sent back again.

English

95

Sing a song of sixpence,
A pocket full of rye;
Four and twenty blackbirds
Baked in a pie.

When the pie was opened,
The birds began to sing;
Wasn't that a dainty dish
To set before the king?

The king was in his counting house,
Counting out his money;
The queen was in the parlour,
Eating bread and honey.

The maid was in the garden,
Hanging out the clothes,
Along came a blackbird
And pecked off her nose.

English

I had a little nut tree,
Nothing would it bear
But a silver nutmeg
And a golden pear;
The King of Spain's daughter
Came to visit me,
All for the sake
Of my little nut tree.
I skipp'd over water,
I danced over sea
And all the birds in the air
Couldn't catch me.

English

97

The lion and the unicorn
Were fighting for the crown;
The lion beat the unicorn
All round the town.

Some gave them white bread,
And some gave them brown;
Some gave them plum cake
And drummed them out of town.

English

98

Yankee Doodle came to town,
A-riding on a pony;
He stuck a feather in his cap,
And called it macaroni.

Yankee Doodle, keep it up.
Yankee Doodle dandy;
Mind the music and the step,
And with the girls be handy.

Father and I went down to camp,
Along with Captain Gooding,
And there we saw the men and boys
As thick as hasty pudding.

And there was Captain Washington
Upon a slapping stallion,
A-giving orders to his men,
I guess there was a million.

American

Oh, the grand old Duke of York,
He had ten thousand men;
He marched them up to the top of the hill,
And he marched them down again.
And when they were up, they were up,
And when they were down, they were down,
And when they were only half-way up,
They were neither up nor down.

English

As I was going out one day,
My head fell off and ran away
But when I saw that it was gone,
I picked it up and put it on.

And when I got into the street,
A fellow cried: "LOOK AT YOUR FEET!"
I looked at him and sadly said:
"I've LEFT THEM BOTH ASLEEP IN BED!"

American

One fine day in the middle of the night,
Two dead men got up to fight,
BACK to BACK they faced each other,
Drew their swords and shot each other.
A blind man came to see fair play,
A dumb man came to shout hurray.

English

Simple Simon met a pieman,
Going to the fair;
Says Simple Simon to the pieman,
Let me taste your ware.

Says the pieman to Simple Simon,
Show me first your penny;
Says Simple Simon to the pieman,
Indeed I have not any.

Simple Simon went a-fishing,
For to catch a whale;
All the water he had got,
Was in his mother's pail.

Simple Simon went to look
If plums grew on a thistle;
He pricked his fingers very much,
Which made poor Simon whistle.

He went for water in a sieve
But soon it all ran through;
And now poor Simple Simon
Bids you all adieu.

English

104

As I was going to St Ives,
I met a man with seven wives,
Every wife had seven sacks,
Every sack had seven cats,
Every cat had seven kits:
Kits, cats, sacks and wives,
How many were going to St Ives?

English

Dickery, dickery, dare,
The pig flew up in the air;
The man in brown
Soon brought him down,
Dickery, dickery, dare.

English

Miss Mary Mack, Mack, Mack
All dressed in black, black, black
With silver buttons, buttons, buttons
All down her back, back, back.
She asked her mother, mother, mother
For fifty cents, cents, cents
To see the elephant, elephant, elephant
Jump over the fence, fence, fence.
He jumped so high, high, high
He reached the sky, sky, sky
And didn't get back, back, back
Till the Fourth of July.

African American/Caribbean clapping song

107

There was a crooked man,
And he walked a crooked mile,
He found a crooked sixpence
Against a crooked stile;
He bought a crooked cat,
Which caught a crooked mouse,
And they all lived together
In a little crooked house.

English

108

Doctor Foster went to Gloucester
In a shower of rain;
He stepped in a puddle,
Right up to his middle,
And never went there again.

English

A sunshiny shower,
Won't last half an hour.

English

W hether the weather be fine
Or whether the weather be not,
Whether the weather be cold,
Or whether the weather be hot,
We'll weather the weather,
Whatever the weather,
Whether we like it or not.

Anglo-American

Rain, rain, go away,
Come again another day,
Little Johnny wants to play.
Rain, rain, go to Spain,
Never show your face again.

English

Red sky at night,
Shepherd's delight;
Red sky in the morning,
Shepherd's warning.

English

Ladybird
Will it be rain or fair?
If it's rain, fall from my hand,
If it's fair, then fly.

Welsh

Rain before seven,
Fine before eleven.

English

January brings the snow,
Makes the feet and fingers glow.

February brings the rain,
Thaws the frozen lake again.

March brings breezes, loud and shrill,
Stirs the dancing daffodil.

April brings the primrose sweet,
Scatters daisies at our feet.

May brings flocks of pretty lambs,
Skipping by their fleecy dams.

June brings tulips, lilies, roses,
Fills the children's hands with posies.

Hot July brings cooling showers,
Apricots and gillyflowers.

August brings the sheaves of corn,
Then the harvest home is borne.

Clear September brings blue skies,
Goldenrod and apple pies.

Fresh October brings the pheasant,
Then to gather nuts is pleasant.

Dull November brings the blast,
Makes the leaves go whirling fast.

Chill December brings the sleet,
Blazing fire and Christmas treat.

English

Snow, snow faster

Ally-ally-blaster

The old woman's plucking her geese

Selling the feathers a penny a piece.

English

The north wind doth blow
And we shall have snow
And what will poor Robin do then
Poor thing?
He'll sit in the barn
And keep himself warm
And hide his head under his wing
Poor thing

English

Christmas is a coming.
The geese are getting fat.
Please to put a penny in the old man's hat.
If you haven't got a penny,
A ha'penny will do.
If you haven't got a ha'penny
Then God bless you.

English

116

Little Jack Horner
Sat in the corner,
Eating his Christmas pie;
He put in his thumb,
And pulled out a plum
And said "what a good boy am I!"

English

117

Jon Klassen

In spring I look gay
Decked in comely array,
In summer more clothing I wear,
When colder it grows,
I fling off my clothes,
And in winter quite naked appear.

English

A tree

I whistle without lips,
I fly without wings,
I clap without hands
And touch all living things.

Latino

The wind

Lives in winter,
Dies in summer,
And grows with its roots upwards.

English

An icicle

There was a young farmer of Leeds
Who swallowed six packets of seeds.
It soon came to pass
He was covered with grass,
And he couldn't sit down for the weeds.

English

Thistle-seed, thistle-seed,
Fly away, fly,
The hair on your body
Will take you up high;
Let the wind whirl you
Around and around,
You'll not hurt yourself
When you fall to the ground.

Chinese American

121

Puss came dancing out of a barn
With a pair of bagpipes under her arm;
She could sing nothing but, Fiddle cum fee
The mouse has married the bumble-bee.
Pipe, cat – dance, mouse –
We'll have a wedding at our good house.

English

Tom, he was a piper's son,
He learnt to play when he was young,
But all the tunes that he could play
Was 'Over the hills and far away'.
Over the hills and a great way off,
The wind shall blow my topknot off.

English

Laurie Stansfield

All the baby chicks say
Cheep, cheep, cheep
When they're cold and hungry,
When they want to sleep.

Mother Hen goes hunting
To find them wheat and corn.
Then she wraps her wings around them
To keep them safe 'til morn.

Latino

Baa, baa, black sheep,
Have you any wool?
Yes, sir, yes, sir,
Three bags full.
One for the master,
And one for the dame,
And one for the little boy
Who lives down the lane.

English

This little cow eats grass,

This little cow eats hay,

This little cow drinks water,

This little cow runs away,

And this little cow does nothing
But just lie down all day.

Chinese American

Rub-a-dub-dub,
Three men in a tub,
And how do you think they got there?
The butcher, the baker,
The candlestick-maker,
They all jumped out of a rotten potato,
'Twas enough to make a man stare.

English

There was, was, was
a little boat, boat, boat
which never, never, never
learned to float, float, float.

Weeks and weeks and weeks and weeks
and weeks and weeks went by.
It couldn't float - it wouldn't even
try, try, try.

And if this silly story doesn't
sink, sink, sink,
we'll have to tell it one more time,
I think, think, think.

Latino

Three wise men of Gotham
Went to sea in a bowl;
And if the bowl had been stronger.
My tale had been longer.

English

Lucy Cousins

127

Oh, the train pulled in the station.
   The bell was ringing wet.
The train ran by the depot,
   And I think it's running yet.

'Twas midnight on the ocean.
   Not a streetcar was in sight.
The sun and moon were shining,
   And it rained all day that night.

'Twas a summer day in winter,
   And the snow was raining fast
As a barefoot boy with shoes on
   Stood sitting on the grass.

Oh, I jumped into the river
   Just because it had a bed.
I took a sheet of water
   For to cover up my head.

Oh, the rain makes all things beautiful,
   The flowers and grasses, too,
If the rain makes all things beautiful,
   Why didn't it rain on you?

American

Who built the ark?
Noah, Noah!
Who built the ark?
Brother Noah built the ark.

Now didn't old Noah build the ark?
He built it out of hickory bark.
He built it long, both wide and tall,
Plenty of room for the large and small.

He found him an axe and hammer too,
Began to cut and began to hew,
And ev'ry time that hammer ring,
Noah shout and Noah sing.

Now in come the animals two by two,
Hippopotamus and kangaroo.
Now in come the animals three by three,
Two big cats and a bumble bee.

Now in come the animals four by four,
Two through the window and two through
    the door.
Now in come the animals five by five,
Four little sparrows and the redbird's wife.

Now in come the animals six by six,
Elephant laughed at the monkey's tricks.
Now in come the animals seven by seven,
Four from home and the rest from heaven.

And ev'ry time that

Now in come the animals eight by eight,
Some were on time and the others were late.
Now in come the animals nine by nine,
Some was a-shouting and some was a-crying.

Now in come the animals ten by ten,
Five black roosters and five black hens.
Now Noah says, "Go, shut that door,
The rain's started dropping and we can't
    take more."

ammer ring

Noah shout

and Noah sing

Who built the ark?

Noah, Noah.

Who built the ark?

Brother Noah built the ark.

African American spiritual

131

Through the jungle the elephant goes,
Swaying his trunk to and fro,
Munching, crunching, tearing trees,
Stamping seeds, eating leaves.
His eyes are small, his feet are fat,
Hey, elephant, don't behave like that.

Punjabi

At early morn the spiders spin,
And by and by the flies drop in;
And when they call, the spiders say,
Take off your things, and stay all day.

American

Ladybird, ladybird,
Fly away home,
Your house is on fire
And your children all gone;
All except one
And that's little Ann
And she has crept under
The warming pan.

English

Kookaburra sits in the old gum tree,
Merry merry king of the bush is he.
Laugh, kookaburra. Laugh, kookaburra.
Gay your life must be.

Kookaburra sits in the old gum tree,
Eating all the gumdrops he can see.
Stop, kookaburra. Stop, kookaburra.
Leave some there for me.

Australian

134

Fuzzy Wuzzy was a bear;
Fuzzy Wuzzy had no hair.
Fuzzy Wuzzy wasn't fuzzy,
Was he?

American

Fig.(i)

Fig.(ii)

Algy saw a bear.
The bear saw Algy.
The bear grew bulgy.
The bulge was Algy.

American

There was an old woman tossed up in a basket,
Nineteen times as high as the moon;
Where she was going I couldn't but ask it,
For in her hand she carried a broom.

Old woman, old woman, old woman, quoth I,
O whither, O whither, O whither, so high?
To brush the cobwebs off the sky!
Shall I go with thee? Aye, by-and-by.

English

136

Grey goose and gander,
Waft your wings together,
And carry the good king's daughter
Over the one strand river.

English

Hey! diddle, diddle,

The cat and the fiddle,

The cow jumped over the moon.

The little dog laughed

To see such sport,

And the dish ran away with the spoon.

English

Don't talk! Go to sleep!
Eyes shet an' don't you peep!
Keep still, or he jes moans:
"Raw Head an' Bloody Bones!"

African American

W'en de big owl whoops,
An' de screech owl screeks,
An' de win' makes a howlin' sound;
You liddle woolly heads
Had better kiver up
Caze de "hants" is comin' round.

African American

Three little ghostesses,
Sitting on postesses,
Eating buttered toastessses,
Greasing their fistesses,
Up to their wristesses.
Oh, what beastesses
To make such feastesses!

English

Downy white feathers are moving
beneath the sunset and along
the edge of the world.

Tohono O'odham spirit song

On the stone ridge east I go.

On the white road I, red fox, crouching go.

I, red fox, whistle, on the road of stars.

Wintu spirit song

Twinkle, twinkle, little star,
How I wonder what you are!
Up above the world so high,
Like a diamond in the sky.

When the blazing sun is gone,
When he nothing shines upon,
There you show your little light,
Twinkle, twinkle, all the night.

In the dark blue sky you keep,
And often through my curtains peep,
For you never shut your eye,
'Till the sun is in the sky.

As your bright and tiny spark
Lights the traveller in the dark,
Though I know not what you are,
Twinkle, twinkle, little star.

English

Star light, star bright,
First star I see tonight,
I wish I may, I wish I might,
Have the wish I wish tonight.

English

Wee Willie Winkie rins through the toun,
Up stairs and doon stairs in his nicht-gown,
Tirling at the window, cryin' at the lock,
'Are the weans in their bed, for it's now ten o'clock?'

Scottish

Come, let's to bed,
Says Sleepy-head;
Tarry a while, says Slow;
Put on the pot,
Says Greedy-gut,
We'll sup before we go.

English

Up the wooden hill
To Bedfordshire,
Down Sheet Lane,
To Blanket Fair.

English

Go to bed first,
A golden purse;
Go to bed second,
A golden pheasant;
Go to bed third,
A golden bird.

English

Hush-a-bye
Don't you cry
Go to sleep
My little baby.

When you wake
You shall have
All the pretty little horses.

Blacks and bays
Dapples and grays
All the pretty little horses.

Hush-a-bye
Don't you cry
Go to sleep
My little baby.

African American

You are weeping
Little girl, darling girl
You are weary
Little girl, darling girl
Be sad no longer
There is love for you
in the heart of the Father
Little girl, darling girl.

Maori, New Zealand

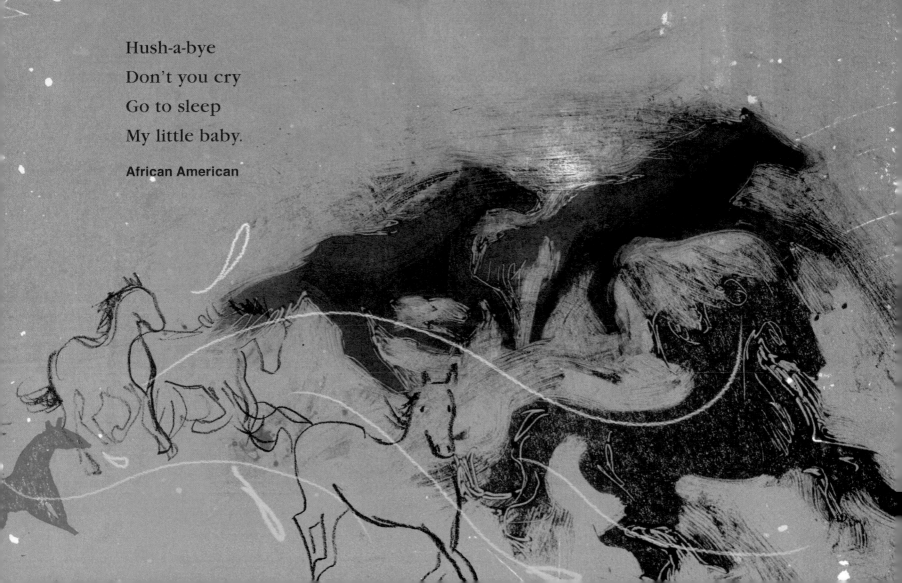

Bed is too small for my tiredness.
Give me a hilltop with trees;
Tuck a cloud up under my chin.
Lord, blow out the moon—please.

Rock me to sleep in a cradle of dreams.

Sing me a lullaby of leaves;

Tuck a cloud up under my chin.

Lord, blow out the moon—please.

American

151

About the Artists

Jessica Ahlberg is the daughter of the acclaimed English writer/illustator duo Allan and Janet Ahlberg. She has illustrated books by her father – *Half a Pig* and *Goldilocks* – as well as Toon Tellegren's enchanting, philosophical animal stories, including the Marsh Award winner, *Letters to Anyone and Everyone*.

Pamela Allen is an award-winning New Zealand author and illustrator, whose 30 picture books include modern classics such as *Mr Archimedes' Bath* and *Who Sank the Boat?*, as well as *Bertie and the Bear* and *Shhh! Little Mouse*.

Meshack Asare is Ghana's foremost writer and illustrator. His children's books, such as *Tawia Goes to Sea* and *Sosu's Call*, have won numerous prizes, including the UNESCO First Prize for Children's and Young People's Literature in the Service of Tolerance.

Nicola Bayley is an English illustrator, whose award-winning picture books – *The Necessary Cat*, *Katje the Windmill Cat*, and *The Mousehole Cat* are noted for their beauty, precision, detail and subtle use of colour.

Ian Beck is an English novelist and artist. An illustrator of folk and fairy tales, he has self-illustrated *The Teddy Robber* and the award-winning *Teddy* series. His children's novels include *The Secret History of Tom Trueheart, Boy Adventurer*.

Jenny Bent is Jamaican, but she lives in England. She has illustrated John Agard's *Calypso Alphabet* and *Wriggle Piggy Toes* as well as her own work, including *How Anansi Captured the Tiger* and *The Green Banana Hunt*.

Caroline Binch is an English author and artist, known for her illustrations for Mary Hoffman's bestselling *Amazing Grace* and its sequels. *Hue Boy*, with Rita Phillips Mitchell, won the Smarties Prize, while *Gregory Cool* was shortlisted for the Kate Greenaway Medal, and *Since Dad Left* won the United Kingdom Book Award.

Ashley Bryan was the first African-American to publish a children's book as both author and illustrator, in 1962. In a career spanning more than 50 years, this artist, writer, anthologist, storyteller, and noted scholar of African and African-American folklore, has created more than 30 picture books and been honoured with numerous awards.

Don Cadoret is an American artist, whose naif story paintings are included in many important public and private collections in the United States, Canada and Europe.

Eric Carle, loved worldwide for *The Very Hungry Caterpillar*, is an award-winning American artist, designer and author of more than 70 books for children. He draws on nature for his subjects. His brightly-coloured, tissue paper collage technique mixed with die-cut pages and other surprising dimensions make tales like *The Very Busy Spider* and *The Very Quiet Cricket* perennial favourites.

Michael Chiago is a Native American Tohono O'odham watercolour artist whose illustrations for the picture book *Sing Down the Rain*, and award-winning paintings, capture the everyday life and ceremonies of his people in Arizona's Sonoran Desert and have been collected and displayed internationally.

Emma Chichester Clark is an English artist who has illustrated books by Roald Dahl, Peter Dickinson, Kevin Crossley-Holland, Michael Morpurgo and Lewis Carroll. She also wrote and illustrated the immensely popular *Blue Kangaroo* series, the *Wagtail Town* books and *Plumdog*.

Rebecca Cobb is an English artist. She has illustrated Helen Dunmore's *The Ferry Boat*, Julia Donaldson's *The Paper Dolls* and Richard Curtis's *The Empty Stocking*, as well as her own *Missing Mummy* and the award-winning *Lunchtime* and *Aunt Amelia*.

Lucy Cousins created the worldwide bestselling *Maisy* series, and won the Bologna Ragazzi Non-fiction Prize for *Maisy's House*. More recent titles from this English illustrator include *Jazzy in the Jungle*, *Hooray for Fish!* and *Yummy*.

Helen Craig is a widely acclaimed English illustrator and author, best known for the *Angelina Ballerina* series which she created with Katherine Holabird. She also illustrated *This Is The Bear* and its sequels with Sarah Hayes, as well as *The Town Mouse and the Country Mouse* and *Rosy's Visitors*.

Nina Crews is a critically acclaimed American author and illustrator, daughter of picture-book makers Donald Crews and the late Ann Jonas. She uses photographs and photo-collages to create books about young urban children, such as *One Hot Summer Day*, *The Neighborhood Mother Goose* and *Jack and the Beanstalk*.

Pippa Curnick is a young English artist and designer and one of

three winners of the Frances Lincoln/Seven Stories Illustration Competition for art students to create a picture for this book. Her illustration was described as '... a riot of colour, life and fun'.

Niki Daly is a renowned South African illustrator and writer, whose picture books, such as *Not So Fast, Songololo*, the *Jamela* series, *Fly, Eagle, Fly* and *The Herd Boy*, celebrate life and the ongoing changes in his country, while subtly challenging social prejudices.

Ted Dewan is an American/British artist whose career has included work in musicals, comedy, as a newspaper cartoonist and an award-winning illustrator. He is best known for his *Crispin* series, *One True Bear*, and the *Bing™ Bunny* series.

Thomas Docherty is a young English artist who illustrates his own stories, including *Little Boat*, which was shortlisted for the Kate Greenaway Medal, and *To the Beach*. He has also illustrated *The Wonderful Adventures of Nils* by Selma Lagerlöf and *The Snatchabook*, created with his wife Helen.

Polly Dunbar, chosen for a Booktrust Best New Illustrator Award, created prize-winning artwork for her own *Penguin* and for Margaret Mahy's *Bubble Trouble*, winner of the Boston Globe Horn Book Award. She illustrated her mother Joyce Dunbar's *Shoe Baby* and the *Tilly and Friends* series, and is a co-founder of Long Nose Puppets.

Michael Foreman is an outstanding contemporary English creator of children's books. His work ranges from his own picture book classic, *Dinosaurs and All that Rubbish*, to illustrated story collections by authors such as the Brothers Grimm, Terry Jones and Michael Morpurgo. He has won the Kate Greenaway Medal twice, for *War Boy: A Country Childhood* and *Long Neck and Thunderfoot*.

Allison Francisco is a young Native American Tohono O'odham artist. She has worked as a curator and artist liaison manager at the new Tohono O'odham Nation Cultural Center and Museum, and has delivered educational projects to young people on the Arizona reservation.

Sarah Garland is an English artist who has written and illustrated more than 40 picture books and stories for young children. She created the much loved preschool series *Coming and Going*, the *Eddie* series and *Azzi in Between*, winner of the inaugural Little Rebels Book Award and an IBBY Honour Book for 2013.

Olivia Lomenech Gill is a Northumbrian artist and award-winning printmaker. Her first book project was to design and illustrate Michael and Clare Morpurgo's poetry anthology, *Where My Wellies Take Me*, which won the English Association 7-11 Picture Book Award.

Gus Gordon is an Australian author and illustrator of more than 70 books for children and young people. His first award-winning picture book, *Wendy*, about a motorcycle-riding stunt chicken, was followed by *Herman and Rosie*, a romance about an alligator and a goat coping with life in New York City.

Bob Graham is an Australian picture-book artist whose stories include *Rose Meets Mr Wintergarden, Buffy, Let's Get a Dog,* and its sequel, *The Trouble with Dogs*. He won the Kate Greenaway Medal for *Jethro Byrde, Fairy Child*, and has been awarded the Australian Children's Book of the Year four times.

Brita Granström and **Mick Manning** are an acclaimed English /Swedish husband and wife team, whose work includes the Smarties Prize-winner, *The World is Full of Babies, Tail-End Charlie, Taff in the Waff*, winner of the English Association Award, *What Mr Darwin Saw*, shortlisted for the Royal Society Young People's Book Award, and *The Beatles*.

Emily Gravett, a Booktrust Best New Illustrator, is one of the most original and experimental English artists creating picture books today. She has won the Kate Greenaway Medal twice, for *Wolves* and *Little Mouse's Big Book of Fears*, and the Boston Globe Horn Book Honor Award for *Wolves*. Her other titles include *Wolf Won't Bite!, Again!,* and *Cave Baby* with Julia Donaldson.

Mini Grey is an English picture book creator, selected for a Booktrust Best New Illustrator Award. She has won the Kate Greenaway Medal for *The Adventures of the Dish and the Spoon* and the Boston Globe Horn Book Award for *Traction Man is Here*. Her fabulously offbeat stories include *The Pea and the Princess, Biscuit Bear* and *Toys in Space*.

Piet Grobler, South African by birth, now lives in England, where he heads the Illustration course at the University of Worcester. An internationally acclaimed designer and illustrator, he has won many prizes for his picture books. His recent books include *Aesop's Fables* with Beverley Naidoo, which won a Parents Choice Silver Award, and *The Magic Bojabi Tree* with Dianne Hofmeyr.

Mark Hearld is a young English artist and printmaker whose work is inspired by the natural world. He works in a range of media: paint, print, collage, textiles and ceramics — illustrating his debut book, Nicola Davies's *A First Book of Nature*, to great acclaim.

Bill Helin/Welaaxum Yout is a designer, engraver, painter, woodcarver, illustrator and storyteller from the Canadian Tsimshian First Nation Gitsees Tribe. His design has travelled into outer space, his woodcarving into creating the world's largest totem pole and canoe, and his storytelling into celebrating Tsimshian mythology and life in a Children's Guided Reading Project for Strong Nations Publishing.

Paul Hess, originally from Australia, now lives in England, where he works as a designer and illustrator. A humorous, surreal edge distinguishes his award-winning artwork for a range of retellings of classic folk and fairy tales including Eric Maddern's *Nail Soup* and *Cow on the Roof* and Kathryn Cave's *Troll Wood*.

Shirley Hughes, OBE, is one of the best loved English creators of picture books. Affectionate and reassuring, her award-winning stories feature the endearing characters Lucy, Tom, Alfie, Annie Rose and Dixie O'Day. She has won the Kate Greenaway Medal twice, for *Dogger* and *Ella's Big Chance*, and the Eleanor Farjeon Award for her outstanding contribution to children's literature.

Pat Hutchins is an English picture-book maker whose inventiveness was first evident in her now classic *Rosie's Walk* (1968). Visual and verbal jokes engage readers in stories like *Good-night, Owl, Titch*, and the Kate Greenaway Award-winning *The Wind Blew*.

Catherine Hyde is an English artist known for her delicate and dreamlike landscape paintings, collected worldwide. Recently she has illustrated Carol Ann Duffy's award-winning modern fairy tale *The Princess's Blanket*, Saviour Pirotta's *The Firebird*, and Jackie Morris's *Little Evie in the Wild Wood*.

Robert Ingpen is a distinguished graphic designer, author and artist, and the only Australian to be awarded the Hans Christian Andersen Medal for Illustration. His internationally admired re-visionings of classic stories include *Treasure Island, The Wind in the Willows, The Wizard of Oz* and *Pinocchio*.

Yasmeen Ismail is an Irish, London-based illustrator and animator, whose versatile use of inks, paints and watercolours, and interest in paper craft, design, typography and collage shines in her first picture book *Time for Bed, Fred* and her drawing book *Inside, Outside, Upside Down*.

Ann James is an award-winning Australian illustrator, who has created artwork for Robin Klein's Penny Pollard series, Margaret Wild's *The Midnight Gang* and Libby Gleeson's Hannah series.

Co-founder of Books Illustrated, she has also won the Pixie O'Harris Award and the Dromkeen Medal for Distinguished Service to Australian Children's Literature.

Sian Jenkins is a young Welsh illustrator who was one of three winners of the Frances Lincoln/Seven Stories Illustration Competition for art students to create a picture for this book. Sian has also developed a series of picture books for the World Wildlife Fund about the realities of animal poaching and deforestation.

Satoshi Kitamura is an internationally acclaimed Japanese picture book author and illustrator. He has created more than 20 books, illustrating the now classic award winning picture book *Angry Arthur*, by Hiawyn Oram, and collaborating with poet John Agard on *The Young Inferno* and *Goldilocks on CCTV*.

Jon Klassen is a Canadian artist and author, who initially worked on animated films such as *Coraline* before turning to book illustration. His startling originality has already seen him win the Canadian Governor General's Award, the Boston Globe Horn Book Award for Mac Barnett's *Extra Yarn* and the Caldecott Medal for *This is Not My Hat*.

John Lawrence is widely recognised as one of the great contemporary English illustrators and wood engravers, winning the prestigious Frances Williams Illustration Award twice. He has illustrated more than 200 books, including *Watership Down, Treasure Island,* and Philip Pullman's His Dark Materials trilogy and *Lyra's Oxford*, as well as his own picture books, such as *This Little Chick*.

Alan Lee is an award-winning English illustrator and film conceptual designer, noted for his work on JRR Tolkien's *Lord of the Rings* and *The Hobbit* and fantasies by Brian Froud, Michael Palin, Peter Dickinson and Joan Aiken. He won the Kate Greenaway Medal for Rosemary Sutcliff's retelling of *The Iliad: Black Ships Before Troy*.

Kate Leiper is a young Scottish artist and illustrator, whose mixed media works in ink and pastels on a variety of papers have been exhibited throughout the UK. Her interest in myth, legend, poetry and ballad shines in her artwork for Teresa Breslin's *An Illustrated Treasury of Scottish Folk and Fairy Tales*.

David Lucas is a celebrated English author and illustrator who was chosen as one of Booktrust's Best New Illustrators. From his first book, *Halibut Jackson*, to his more recent titles, including *Grendel: A Cautionary Tale About Chocolate* and *A Letter for Bear*, Lucas creates fairy tales which communicate his belief that 'the world is a magical place'.

P J Lynch is an award-winning Irish illustrator, noted for his work on folktales and classics such as *East o' the Sun and West o' the Moon* and *A Christmas Carol*. He has won the Kate Greenaway Medal twice, for *The Christmas Miracle of Jonathan Toomey* by Susan Wojciechowski and *Jessie Came from Across the Sea* by Amy Hest.

James Mayhew is an English author, artist and storyteller whose books reflect his passionate advocacy of the arts for young children. His imaginative *Katie* series invites readers to step inside famous paintings come alive, his

Ella Bella Ballerina series explores classic ballets, and other works retell folk tales and stories from opera and Shakespeare.

Jayme McGowan is an American illustrator who creates unique 3-D cut paper diorama images. Her illustrations have appeared in national newspapers, advertising, magazine editorials and retail products as well as animation. Her first picture book, *Bear Finds His Song*, will be published in 2015.

Daniel Minter is an American artist whose paintings, sculpture and illustrations draw on African American and African Diaspora culture. His artwork for children's books includes *The Riches of Oseola McCarty, Seven Spools of Thread: A Kwanzaa Story* and *Ellen's Broom* by Kelly Starling Lyons, winner of the 2013 Coretta Scott King Illustration Award.

Lydia Monks is an award-winning English author and illustrator, known for her distinctive use of collage and colour. She has illustrated more than 40 picture books from her own *I Wish I Was a Dog* to collaborations with Julia Donaldson such as *What the Ladybird Heard* and *The Rhyming Snail*.

Sara Ogilvie, born in Scotland, now living in England, is an internationally acclaimed artist and printmaker who was recently selected for a Booktrust Best New Illustrator Award. A freelance illustrator, her picture books include *Dogs Don't Do Ballet, Rhinos Don't Eat Pancakes* and *The Worst Princess*.

Jerry Pinkney is a distinguished American illustrator. The recipient of numerous awards, including the

Caldecott Medal for *The Lion and the Mouse*, five Caldecott Honors, and five Coretta Scott King Awards, and the Boston Globe Horn Book Award for Julius Lester's *John Henry*, he is the first children's illustrator to be inducted into the American Academy of Arts & Sciences.

Andrew Qappik is a Canadian Inuit graphic artist known for his printmaking and his contribution to the Nunavut Coat of Arms. His prints and book illustrations depict scenes of arctic animals and traditional and contemporary Inuit life, stories and legends. He has received awards from the Royal Canadian Academy of Arts, a Queen Elizabeth Jubilee Medal and a Northwest Territories Medal.

Chris Raschka is an innovative American illustrator, writer and violist whose artwork has been likened to 'visual haiku'. His work ranges from the Caldecott Honor Book *Yo! Yes!* and *Charlie Parker Played Be Bop* to collaborations with Sharon Creech and poetry editor Paul B. Janeczko. He has won the Caldecott Award twice for *The Hello, Goodbye Window* and *A Ball for Daisy*.

Jane Ray is a distinguished English artist, whose visual interpretations of biblical tales and works by authors as varied as Shakespeare, Oscar Wilde, Carol Ann Duffy and Vikram Seth, are internationally admired. Recent books include *Ahmed and the Feather Girl, Zeraffa Giraffa* and *The Emperor's Nightingale and Other Feathery Tales*.

Catherine Rayner is an English author and artist, who now lives in Edinburgh. Chosen for a Booktrust Best New Illustrator Award, she creates picture books inspired by her menagerie of animals, and won a Kate Greenaway Medal for *Harris Finds His Feet*. Her recent works include *Sylvia and Bird*, *Posy* written by Linda Newbery, *Ernest* and *Solomon Crocodile*.

Amy Schwartz is an American illustrator and author, whose outstanding picture books include *Bea and Mr. Jones*, *A Teeny Tiny Baby*, *What James Likes Best*, winner of the Charlotte Zolotow Award, *Dee Dee and Me*, and *Mrs. Moskowitz and the Sabbath Candlesticks*, winner of the National Jewish Book Award.

Axel Scheffler is an award-winning, bestselling German illustrator, now living in England. Known internationally for his humorous collaborations with writer Julia Donaldson from *The Gruffalo* to *Room on the Broom* to *Zog*, he has also written and illustrated a pre-school picture book series about Pip and Posy.

Niamh Sharkey, Ireland's second Children's Laureate (2012-2014), won the Mother Goose Award and the Bisto Book of the Year Award for her first books *The Gigantic Turnip* and *Tales of Wisdom and Wonder*. She illustrated Malachy Doyle's acclaimed *Tales of Ancient Ireland*, and more recently, *The Ravenous Beast*, *Santasaurus* and *I'm a Happy Hugglewug*.

Nick Sharratt is an award-winning English illustrator and author. He has illustrated more than 200 children's books, including 40 picture books of his own. He has collaborated with authors from Julia Donaldson to Michael Rosen. His most famous partnership with Jacqueline Wilson began with *The Story of Tracy Beaker*.

Laurie Stansfield is a young English artist, a recent art school graduate in illustration. A member of an illustrators' collective, Drawn in Bristol, for which she has created greetings cards, she is also learning to scrive.

Holly Sterling, a young Jamaican English artist, is one of three winners of the Frances Lincoln/Seven Stories Illustration Competition for art students to create a picture for this book. Her artwork weaves an African American and a Maori lullaby together 'subtly, freshly, distinctively.' Her first picture book, *15 Things Not to Do With a Baby*, will be published in 2015.

Joel Stewart is an award-winning English author and illustrator. Known for his televised *Adventures of Abney and Teal* and internationally for his *Dexter Bexley* picture books, he has illustrated classics such as *Tales of Hans Christian Andersen* and *Jabberwocky*, and stories by Vivian Schwartz, Julia Donaldson and Michael Rosen.

Emily Sutton is a young English illustrator whose work is influenced by the Yorkshire countryside and artefacts found in museums and antique shops. Fashion items from the Victoria and Albert Museum inspired *Clara Button and the Magical Hat Day* and its sequel, *Clara Button and the Wedding Day Surprise*.

Shaun Tan is an acclaimed Australian writer and illustrator whose picture books for older readers deal with complex social, political, and historical issues: colonial imperialism (*The Rabbits*), depression (*The Red Tree*), difference (the Oscar

winning *The Lost Thing*) and the immigrant experience (*The Arrival*).

Charlotte Voake, Welsh by birth, lives in England. Her work ranges from the award-winning *Ginger* and *Pizza Kittens* to classics such as Eleanor Farjeon's *Elsie Piddock Skips in her Sleep*, poetry by Allan Ahlberg, and narrative information books such as *Caterpillar, Butterfly*, and *A Little Guide to Trees*.

Clara Vulliamy is an English writer and illustrator, known for her picture book series *Lucky Wish Mouse, Martha and the Bunny Brothers*, and *Muffin*. She is collaborating, as illustrator, with her mother, Shirley Hughes, on a 'visually stunning' series of adventure stories for newly independent readers beginning with *Dixie O'Day in the Fast Lane*.

Kevin Waldron, Dublin born, studied art in London and now lives in New York. A Booktrust Best New Illustrator, he won the Bologna Ragazzi Opera Prima Award for his first *Mr Peek* book, *Mr Peek and the Misunderstanding at the Zoo*. He illustrated Michael Rosen's rhyme *Tiny Little Fly* to great acclaim.

Bruce Whatley, born in the UK, is now an Australian author and illustrator of more than 60 picture books. These include the award-winning *The Ugliest Dog in the World, Detective Donut and the Wild Goose Chase* and Jackie French's *Diary of a Wombat*. *Flood* and *The Little Refugee* were CBCA Honour books.

Mo Willems is a celebrated American illustrator who won six Emmy awards as an animator and

writer on *Sesame Street* before creating the Caldecott Honor-winning *Don't Let the Pigeon Drive the Bus!*, *Knuffle Bunny: A Cautionary Tale*, and *Knuffle Bunny Too: A Case of Mistaken Identity*. His *Elephant and Piggie* books have won three Theodor Seuss Geisel Medals.

Marcia Williams is an English artist whose distinctive graphic novel style has introduced young readers to many literary classics. Among her acclaimed retellings are *Mr William Shakespeare's Plays, Charles Dickens and Friends* and *Lizzie Bennet's Diaries*. Historical titles include *Archie's War*.

Petrina Wright, an English artist now living in Spain and Sussex, spent many years in the Cayman Islands. Her paintings echo the vibrant colour of Caribbean life. So, too, does her artwork for Philip Sherlock's *The Illustrated Anansi: Four Caribbean Folktales* and Jill Pickering's *Lizard Got Into the Paint Pots*.

Ed Young is a Chinese born American illustrator of some 80 books for children. His *Lon Po Po: A Red-Riding Hood Story from China* won the Caldecott Medal and the Boston Globe Horn Book Award, which he also received for *Seven Blind Mice* and *Yeh Shen*. Recent work includes *Night-time Ninja* and *The House Baba Built: An Artist's Childhood in China*.

Pamela Zagarenski is an American artist and illustrator who creates rich, detailed mixed media worlds in her paintings and picture book artwork. Her titles include Mary Logue's *Sleep Like a Tiger* and Janet Sidman's *Red Sings from Treetops: A Year in Colour* – both Caldecott Honor Books.

Index of First Lines

A

A riddle, a riddle, as I suppose	64
A sunshiny shower	110
A was an apple pie	48
A wee little boy	34
Abna Babna	56
Algy saw a bear	135
All the baby chicks say	124
Alas! Alas! For Miss Mackay!	72
An eagle marching on a line	64
As I was going out one day	102
As I was going to St Ives	105
At early morn the spiders spin	133

B

Baa, baa, black sheep	124
Baby and I	22
Bed is too small for my tiredness	150
Betty Botter bought some butter	66
Boys and girls come out to play	54
Brow bender	26

C

Christmas is a coming	116
Come, let's to bed	146

D

Dance, little baby, dance up high	14
Dance to your daddy	15
Dickery, dickery, dare	107
Diddle diddle dumpling, my son John	36

Dis lickle pig go a markit	87
Doctor Foster went to Gloucester	109
Don't talk! Go to sleep!	140
Downy white feathers are moving	142

E

Eena, deena, dina, do	56
Earkin-Hearkin	26
Entry, kentry, cutry, corn	57

F

Fuzzy Wuzzy was a bear	135

G

Gay go up and gay go down	90
Georgie Porgie, pudding and pie	41
Go to bed first	147
Goosey, goosey, gander (English)	80
Goosey Goosey Gander (Australian)	80
Gregory Griggs, Gregory Griggs	89
Grey goose and gander	137

H

Hannah Bantry, in the pantry	70
Hector Protector was dressed all in green	95
Here am I	37
Hey! diddle, diddle	139
Hickory, dickory, dock	79
Higglety, pigglety, pop!	84
How shall I begin my song	10
Hush-a-bye	149

Hush-a-bye, baby 18

Hush, little baby, don't say a word 16

I

I eat my peas with honey 63

I had a little husband 75

I had a little nut tree 97

I scream, you scream 62

I whistle without lips 119

If all the world were paper 63

In marble walls as white as milk 65

In spring I look gay 118

Inty minty tibblety fig 57

It has eyes and a nose 65

It's raining, it's pouring 81

J

Jack and Jill 46

Jack be nimble 77

Jack Sprat could eat no fat 71

Janey Mac, me shirt is black 37

January brings the snow 112

Jerry Hall 77

K

Knock at the door 27

Kookaburra sits in the old gum tree 134

L

Ladybird 111

Ladybird, ladybird 133

Lickle Miss Julie 38

Little baby, sleep 19

Little Bo-peep has lost her sheep 44

Little Boy Blue 45

Little Jack Horner 117

Little Miss Muffet (English) 38

Little Miss Muffet (Australian) 39

Little Miss Tuckett 39

Little Nancy Etticoat 64

Little Sally Water 58

Lives in winter 119

M

Mary, Mary, quite contrary 36

Miss Lucy had a baby 42

Miss Mary Mack, Mack, Mack 107

Monday's child is fair of face 32

Moses supposes his toeses are roses 28

Mosquito one 60

Mrs Mason 88

O

Oh, the grand old Duke of York 101

Oh, the train pulled in the station 128

Old King Cole 94

Old Mother Hubbard 82

On the stone ridge east I go 143

One fine day in the middle of the night 103

One, two, buckle my shoe 50

One, two, three, four, five 52

P

Pat-a-cake, pat-a-cake 23

Pease porridge hot 62

Peter, Peter, pumpkin-eater 74

Peter Piper picked a peck of pickled peppers	67
Polly put the kettle on	35
Poussie at the fireside	69
Puss came dancing out of a barn	122
Pussy cat, pussy cat, where have you been?	93

R

Rain before seven	111
Rain, rain, go away	111
Red sky at night	111
Ring-a-ring o' roses	55
Roses are red	29
Rub-a-dub-dub	126

S

Simple Simon met a pieman	104
Sing, sing	68
Sing a song of sixpence	96
Six little mice sat down to spin	79
Snow, snow faster	114
Someone would like to have you for her child	13
Star light, star bright	145

T

The lion and the unicorn	98
The little girl was born to gather wild roses	20
The north wind doth blow	115
The Queen of Hearts	92
There once was a fish	53
There was a crooked man	108
There was a little girl	40
There was a young farmer of Leeds	120

There was an old woman who lived in a shoe	76
There was an old woman tossed up in a basket	136
There was, was, was	127
This little cow eats grass	125
This little pig went to market	87
Thistle-seed, thistle-seed	121
Three blind mice	78
Three little ghostesses	141
Three wise men of Gotham	127
Through the jungle the elephant goes	132
To market, to market	84
Tom, he was a piper's son	123
Tom, Tom, the piper's son	85
Twinkle, twinkle, little star	144

U

Up the wooden hill	147

W

We keep a dog to watch the house	31
Wee Willie Winkie rins through the toun	146
W'en de big owl whoops	140
What are little boys made of, made of	30
When I was a little boy	73
Whether the weather be fine	110
Who built the ark?	130

Y

Yankee Doodle came to town	100
You are weeping	149
You thumb there, wake up!	24

seven stories

National Centre for Children's Books

Every child – every family – deserves the chance to share books. Reading together builds happy memories and instills a joy in words.

By buying this book, you have supported the work of Seven Stories, National Centre for Children's Books in Britain. Seven Stories is an educational charity that saves, celebrates and shares Britain's outstanding literary heritage for children. The idea was born in Newcastle upon Tyne in the Northeast of England, and this is where our centre opened in 2005. Seven Stories' home is an imaginatively converted Victorian warehouse with seven floors. Our name plays with the idea that there are just seven story plots in all the world and thousands of ways to tell them.

We are the only place in Britain dedicated to the art of children's books and the joy of reading, and one of just a few such museums in the world. We are saving our literary heritage by building an internationally important collection of artwork, manuscripts and archives of Britain's acclaimed writers and illustrators for children, from the 1930s to the present day. We celebrate this treasure trove by creating playful and immersive exhibitions, which tour, along with inclusive learning and outreach programmes. We explore how books are made – from first scribbles, drafts and roughs to the finished book. We share this creativity by encouraging children, young people and adults to voice their own thoughts, ideas and stories. All of the artwork in this book has a home at Seven Stories, where it is inventively used to inspire children and the next generation of talented illustrators.

Everything we do aims to awaken curiosity and imagination in the hope that, regardless of age, background or ability, the children and adults we meet will go on to enjoy a lifetime enriched by reading and the incredible journeys we embark on when we 'step inside' a book.

Find out more at www.sevenstories.org.uk

Kate Edwards
Chief Executive

Supported using public funding by
**ARTS COUNCIL
ENGLAND**

Sources

In selecting rhymes and verses to include in this collection, I consulted many sources - literary and personal. *The Oxford Dictionary of Nursery Rhymes*, edited by Iona and Peter Opie, Oxford, Oxford University Press, 1951, reprinted with corrections 1952, and *The Annotated Mother Goose*, William S and Cecil Baring-Gould, New York, New American Library, 1967, often served as starting reference points, especially for the fascinating histories behind many of the nursery rhymes and their variants. So too did Albert Jack's *Pop Goes the Weasel: the Secret Meanings of Nursery Rhymes*, London, Allen Lane, 2008.

Other general sources include:
The Project Gutenberg eBook of Chinese Mother Goose Rhymes, translated and illustrated by Isaac Taylor Headland of Peking University, Fleming H. Revell Company, New York, Chicago, Toronto, 1900, www.gutenberg.org/files/40425/40425-h/40425-h.htm

The Project Gutenberg eBook of Negro Folk Rhymes, with a study by Thomas W Talley, New York, The Macmillan Company, 1922, www.gutenberg.org/files/27195/27195-h/27195-h.htm

Every effort has been made to trace and acknowledge sources, but if any have been inadvertently omitted, I and the Publishers will be pleased to be informed.

Sources for Individual Rhymes
An eagle marching on a line: *Mother Goose on the Rio Grande*, Frances Alexander, ill Charlotte Baker, Chicago, Passport Books, 1997.

Dis lickle pig go a market and Lickle Miss Julie: *Jamaica Maddah Goose*, ed. Louise Bennett, Jamaica School of Art, Kingston, 1981.

White Feathers Along the Edge of the World and In the Blue Night : *Papago Music*, Frances Densmore, Washington, D. C., Bureau of American Ethnology, Bulletin 90, 1929.

I whistle without: *Grandmother's Nursery Rhymes*: *Lullabies, Tongue Twisters and Riddles from South America, (Las Nanas de Abuelita)*, compiled by Nelly Palacio Jaramillo, illustrated by Elivia, Henry Holt and Company, New York, 1994.

Goosey, Goosey, Gander and Little Miss Muffet, Robert Holden, *Twinkle, Twinkle, Southern Cross: The Forgotten Folklore of Australian Nursery Rhymes*, Canberra: National Library of Australia, 1992. www.nla.gov.au/.../files/twinkletwinklesoutherncross.pdf

Mosquito one: *Down by the River: Afro-Caribbean Rhymes, Games and Songs for Children*, compiled by Grace Hallworth, ill. Caroline Binch, William Heinemann Ltd., London, 1996. Reissued by Frances Lincoln Children's Books 2011.

Poussie at the Fireside and Wee Willie Winkie: *Scottish Nursery Rhymes*, selected and edited by Norah and William Montgomerie, Chambers, Edinburgh, 1985.

Song of Red Fox: *The Project Gutenberg Creation Myths of Primitive America*, Jeremiah Curtin, Boston, Little Brown and Company, 1898; www.gutenberg.org/files/39106/39106-h/39106-h.htm

There was, was, was: *¡Pío Peep!, Traditional Spanish Nursery Rhymes*, Selected by Alma Flor Ada & F. Isabel Campoy, English adaptations by Alice Schertle, ill Vivi Escriva, New York, HarperCollins, 2003; Spanish compilation copyright ©Alma Flor Ada & F. Isabel Campoy; English Adaptations ©Alice Schertle

Lullaby for a Girl, Marius Barbeau, 'Tsimshian songs', in *The Tsimshian: Their Arts and Music*, by Viola E. Garfield; Paul S. Wingert; Marius Barbeau. Edited By Marian W. Smith, Washington D.C., American Ethnological Society, XVIII, 1951, p.145, song.no 56, also at: books.google.ca/...Tsimshian_Their_Arts_and_Music.html.: also *A Cry from the Earth: Music of the North American Indians*, John Bierhorst, New York, Four Winds Press, 1979.

You thumb there: *A Phonetical Study of the Eskimo Language*, William Thalbitzer, Meddelelser om Gronland 31. Copenhagen, 1904. archive.org/stream/phoneticalstudyo00thal/phoneticalstudyo00thal_djvu.txt

Sources for illustrations
Elephant, p.132, *Animals Animals* Illustrated by Eric Carle. Illustration copyright ©1989 by Eric Carle. All rights reserved. Used with permission.

Spider, p.133, *The Very Busy Spider* by Eric Carle. Copyright ©1985 by Eric Carle. All rights reserved. Used with permission.

Ladybird, p.133, *The Grouchy Ladybug* by Eric Carle. Copyright ©1977 by Eric Carle. All rights reserved. Used with permission.

With grateful thanks for their help and support
Kate Edwards and the Seven Stories' team and Helena Mulhearn, Diverse Voices Co-ordinator, for their enthusiastic and practical input into creating this collection; Ashley Bryan, artist, for opening his extensive personal library to me and introducing me to important collections of African American and Caribbean verse and rhyme; Tanya Barben, Senior Librarian, Rare Books & Special Collections, University of Cape Town, South Africa for finding South African rhymes to include; Terrol Dew Johnson, artist and President and C.E.O. of Tohono O'odham Community Action (TOCA), Sells, Arizona, USA, and Rowena House, Execuitve Director, and Pascale Arpin, Co-ordinator of Arts Programing, at Nunavut Arts and Crafts Association, Iqaluit, Nunavut, Canada for facilitating contributions to this collection by a Tohono O'odham and an Inuit artist; my family - Tom, Anthony, Judi, and John, my brother John and Marcia, and my cousins Marion and Constance - for their ideas, wisdom, advice and patience; my editor Janetta Otter-Barry, and designers Judith Escreet and Andrew Watson for believing in and delivering this project so splendidly; and all the illustrators whose generosity and artistry made this book possible.